THE Sound IN THE Basement

By John Micklos, Jr.

Illustrated by Eric Hamilton

First State Press

ISBN 10: 0-9964315-0-0

ISBN 13: 978-0-9964315-0-7

Production Date: August 2015
Printed in the United States

Published by First State Press
4142 Ogletown-Stanton Rd., #306
Newark, DE 19713

Book and cover design by Stephanie Fotiadis

Set in Avenir Next Condensed Medium / 15pt.

About the Author

John Micklos, Jr., is the author of more than 20 books, ranging from poetry books for young readers to history, biography, and social studies titles for elementary and secondary students. He loves to visit schools to talk about writing and to conduct writing workshops with students. To learn more, visit www.JohnMicklosWriter.com.

About the Illustrator

Eric L. Hamilton is an artist who lives in New York City, who has illustrated two other books for young readers. He received his Bachelor's and Master's degrees at the School of Visual Arts. He still remembers his first time going down into the basement alone and being disappointed that there were no monsters down there after all.

Dedications

For everyone who has ever overcome fears, and for all those people who helped me face mine.

JM

To Liv and Dad, for believing in my overly imaginative story-doodling as a kid and encouraging me to do it for a living. To Anastasia, Ben, Camilla, Campbell, Grayson, Jack, James, Joni, Laz, Mira and Sash, Nathaniel, Nithya and Tyler, Stella, Vlad, and Winston. And, to everyone and anyone who went into their own personal dark and scary basement … only to come out braver and wiser.

EH

David peeked down into the basement. "You know where the bag of dog food is, don't you?" Mom asked as she made sandwiches for lunch.

"Yes, it's on the shelf." David's voice shook a little.
The shelf stood near a pile of empty boxes in the darkest, loneliest corner of the dark, lonely basement. He had never gone into the basement alone before.

Mom seemed to sense he was frightened. She smiled and patted his shoulder.

"There's nothing to be afraid of down there, " she said. "But if you want company, take Skippy along."

Skippy was his puppy.

"I haven't seen Skippy all morning," David said. "He's probably asleep under the bed. Besides, he wouldn't help. He's scared of everything."

David paused as he reached the bottom of the stairs. A single light bulb pierced the shadows that covered most of the basement. A ray of sunlight trickled in through a small window near the top of the far wall.

The shelf with the dog food stood in the far corner of
the basement. David walked slowly toward it. Then he
heard a low, muffled sound. It was a *moany* sound,
a *groany* sound, a *chill-you-to-the-boney* sound.

David shivered and looked around. He wished Skippy were with him. It wouldn't be as scary if they could be scared together.

He thought about running back upstairs, but he didn't want Mom to know how frightened he was. Then he thought about the story of David and Goliath. He remembered how the brave shepherd boy had fought the giant when everyone else was afraid. He wanted to be that brave, too.

Over by the washing machine, David saw a small, dark figure leaning against the wall. "A mummy!" he exclaimed.

David started to run, but then he thought of the shepherd boy armed with only a sling, and he knew what he had to do. He didn't have a sling, so he picked up a shoe from the floor and flung it at the mummy. The dark figure fell to the floor with a crash.

But it wasn't a mummy at all. It was only the laundry basket and Dad's golf clubs.

"David, are you all right?" Mom called from upstairs. "What happened?"

"I just knocked over Dad's golf clubs. I'm fine."

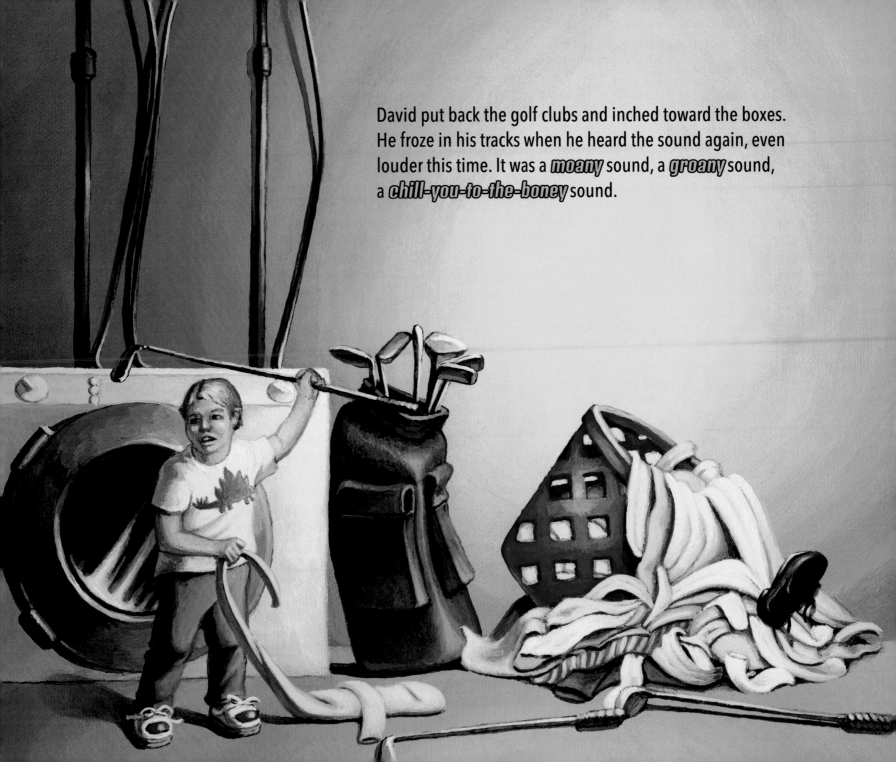

David put back the golf clubs and inched toward the boxes. He froze in his tracks when he heard the sound again, even louder this time. It was a *moany* sound, a *groany* sound, a *chill-you-to-the-boney* sound.

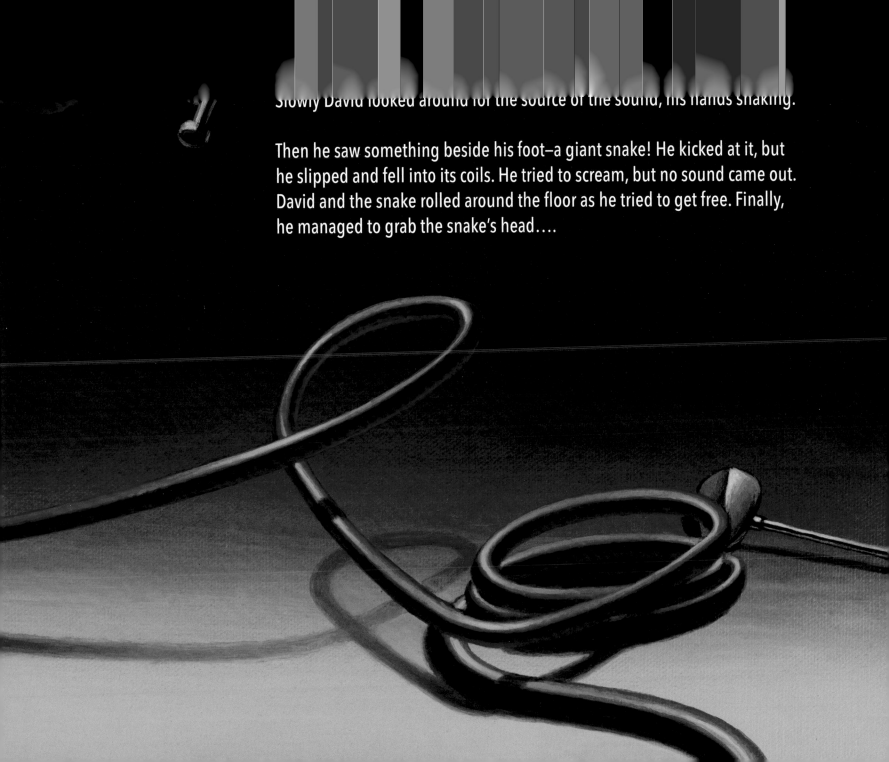

Slowly David looked around for the source of the sound, his hands shaking.

Then he saw something beside his foot—a giant snake! He kicked at it, but he slipped and fell into its coils. He tried to scream, but no sound came out. David and the snake rolled around the floor as he tried to get free. Finally, he managed to grab the snake's head....

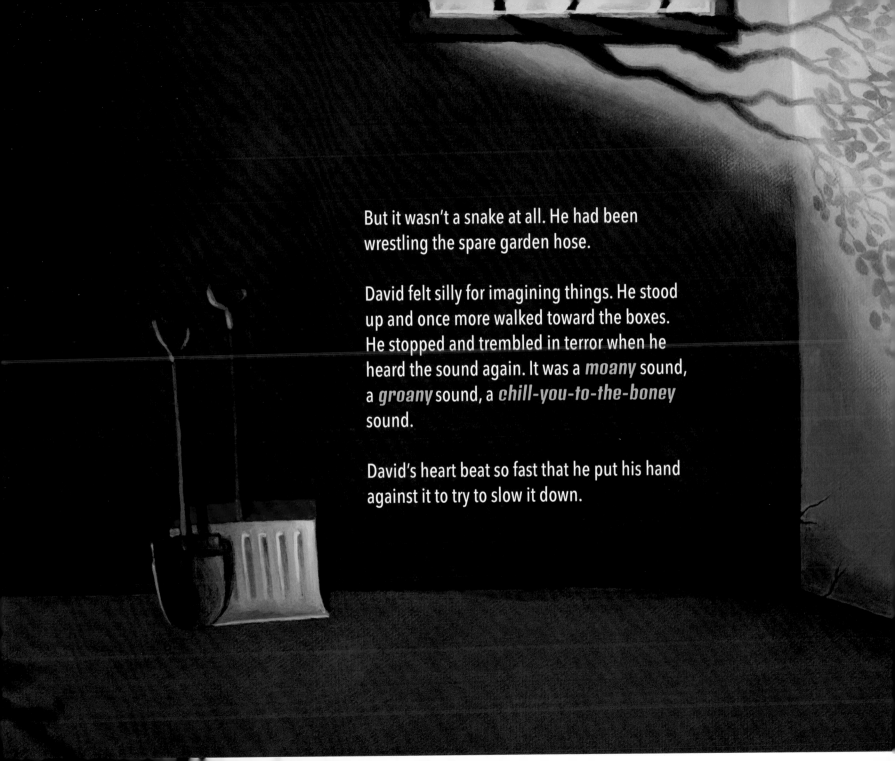

But it wasn't a snake at all. He had been wrestling the spare garden hose.

David felt silly for imagining things. He stood up and once more walked toward the boxes. He stopped and trembled in terror when he heard the sound again. It was a *moany* sound, a *groany* sound, a *chill-you-to-the-boney* sound.

David's heart beat so fast that he put his hand against it to try to slow it down.

A shadow moved along the wall behind the furnace.
"A burglar!" David gasped. He thought about running,
but then he remembered the brave shepherd boy.
David walked back, picked up one of Dad's golf clubs,
and tip-toed toward the moving shadow.

By the time he reached the furnace, David was shaking. He swung the golf club, and it smashed against the wall. The shadow kept moving. He swung again, and the club crashed into the wall again.

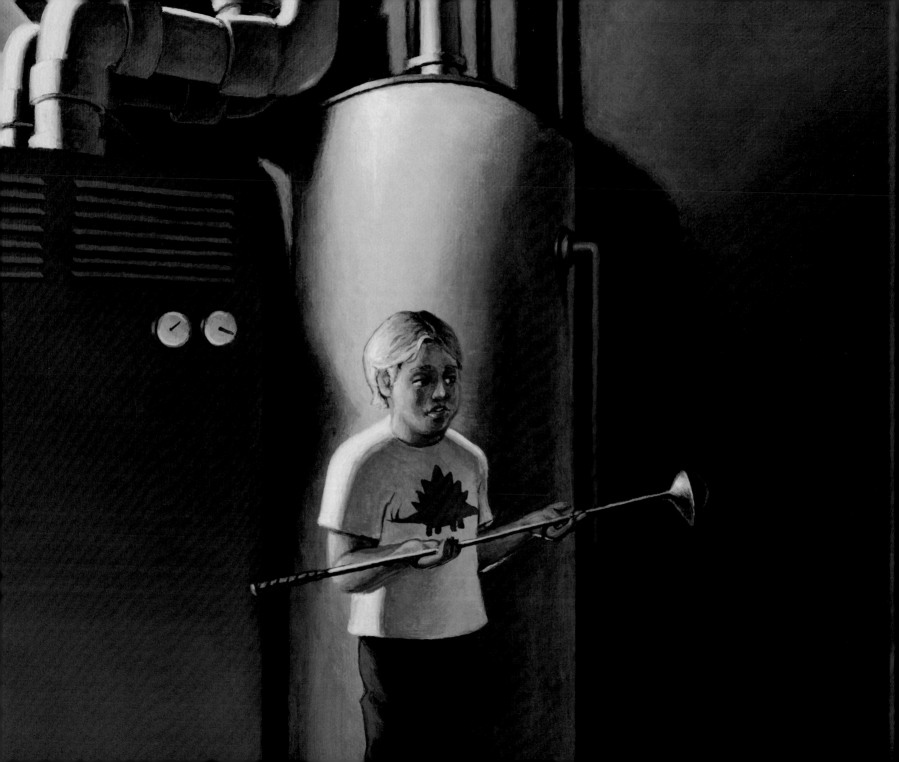

wasn't bent.

"David!" Mom yelled. "What's going on down there? Are you all right?"

"I'm fine."

"Please stop playing around and get that bag of dog food. Lunch is almost ready."

"All right, Mom."

David once again walked toward the shelf holding the dog food. He felt braver now. He had only imagined the mummy, the snake, and the burglar. Maybe Mom was right. Maybe there really wasn't anything scary in the basement after all. But as he neared the shelf, he heard the sound again. This time it seemed like it was right beside him. It was a *moany* sound, a *groany* sound, a *chill-you-to-the-boney* sound.

Then he saw it. One of the empty boxes was moving!
It shook. It rattled. It started to move across the floor,
then stopped. The sound came from inside—a muffled
and ghostly sound.

David froze for a moment. He thought about running upstairs and getting Mom. Then he remembered the brave shepherd boy David facing the giant. He decided he could be that brave, too. He closed his eyes, took a deep breath, and pounced on the box. "Come on out, whatever you are!" he said in a shaky voice. He lifted the box with trembling fingers. Underneath was…

...Skippy!

David fell to the floor, laughing with relief.
Skippy jumped on him and licked his face.

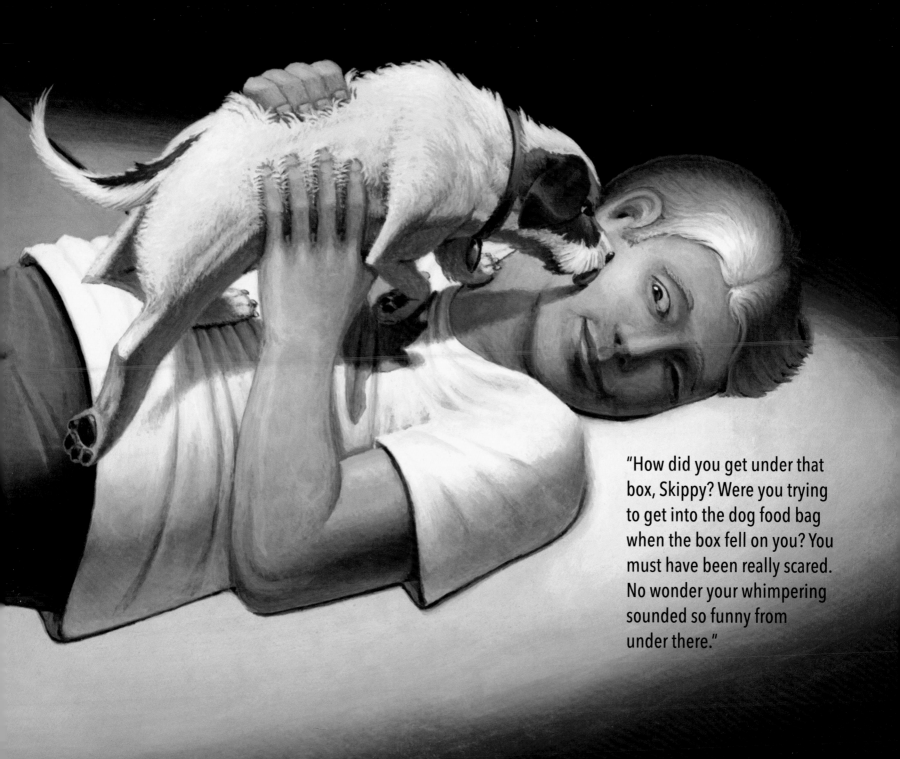

"How did you get under that box, Skippy? Were you trying to get into the dog food bag when the box fell on you? You must have been really scared. No wonder your whimpering sounded so funny from under there."

"Come on, Skippy," David said.
"We'll take the dog food up to Mom."

Together, they ran up the stairs.

"I see you found Skippy to go along with you," Mom said as David proudly handed her the dog food bag. "Now that wasn't so hard, was it?"

David paused. He wondered whether to tell Mom how scared he had been. He wondered whether to tell her about the mummy, the snake, and the burglar. He wondered whether to tell her about the spooky sound and how he found Skippy under the box.

In the end, David just shook his head and smiled at Skippy. "You can send me down into the basement any time."